Mountain Miracle
A Nativity Story

by Álvaro Correa, LC
Illustrated by Gloria Lorenzo

CIRCLE
PRESS

First U.S. edition published by Circle Press, a division of Circle Media, Inc.

Illustrations by Gloria Lorenzo

CIP data is on file with the Library of Conress

ISBN: 978-1-933271-23-1

PRINTED IN THE UNITED STATES OF AMERICA

5 4 3 2 1

To my parents, my brothers and sisters,

to everyone with whom I have shared each Christmas,

to all parish priests and families.

TABLE OF CONTENTS

INTRODUCTION

Each Christmas story invites us to take a step further into the stable at Bethlehem. It is true that the imaginative events of the story have their own value, but the really important work of art is within the heart of each reader—in his or her own love and faith.

Mountain Miracle is the story of a great adventure involving two children, Martin and Beth, who are invited by their pastor, Father Anthony, to play the parts of St. Joseph and the Blessed Virgin Mary after Midnight Mass on Christmas Eve. The original plan was to use a toy figure for the Baby Jesus, but the priest accepted Beth's idea to ask a family to bring a real baby for the presentation. The children tried hard, but no baby could be found. The children's strong faith and loving tenacity is rewarded, and they receive a special miracle from heaven by holding in their arms on Christmas night the real Baby Jesus.

The story takes place in a mountain village where everything is carpeted with snow. According to an old village tradition dating back to the very first pastor, Father Anthony had decided that the Nativity scene would be "almost entirely natural" in an open cave by a stone wall leading into the village.

The chapters of the story are the steps in time of the adventure which begins when Martin is woken up by his audacious little brother, and the story finishes when Beth and he go off to bed with their hearts filled with gratitude and joy. The whole story happens in one day: the 24th of December.

There is a space too for the reader among the characters of the story, and each of us is invited to join in the conversations of the different characters. Christmas Eve is a wonderful opportunity to meet the Baby Jesus who is to be found in the arms of his Mother, the Blessed Virgin, and in the loving care of St. Joseph. How marvelous it is that we can take this journey every year!

Alvaro Correa, LC
Christmas 2008

Morning on the Mountain

"The rooster has woken up early!" thought Martin, as he covered his face with is pillow. He tried to go back again to the magical land of dreams, but the first rays of sunlight made all those dreams disappear and the colorful scenes fade away. The cock crowed again, and this time a voice nearer to him rang in his ears.

"Martin, aren't you up yet?" asked Alex, his younger brother, once again playing the prank of putting a frog ("Freddie") between the sheets of Martin's bed.

"Alex!" shouted Martin, and with one effort threw the blankets, sheets, pillow, and frog—who, by now well accustomed to this treatment, gave a few jumps and landed again in the hands of his friend Alex. "Someday I'm going to invade your bed with an army of spiders!"

"You always say that, but you never will, because I always get up before you," answered his little brother, who then escaped at full speed.

Martin, dressed in his blue pajamas which had been a birthday present, pursued his brother and stopped his getaway, laughing as he did. Alex knew that the arms of a good brother like Martin would never harm him, and that trust also benefited Freddie the frog. Just then the rooster crowed again, and with the cries of the two boys and an occasional croak from Freddie, it could be said that the trio had started that special day with a suitable song of praise.

The smoke fom the chimney of their house spiraled upwards

until it disappeared into waffery wisps, while the snow covered the countryside just like a shock of white hair. Even the fronts of the stone houses seemed to stretch out fingers to trap the falling snow-flakes and affix them like medals of honor.

Martin's family was not the only one to be awake. There was activity in all of the houses in the village. The same excitement was running through the hearts of all, both children and grownups: "This evening is Christmas Eve, and tomorrow is Christmas!"

There remained only a few hours before the most beautiful star of the year returned again to shorten the night and to show the way to adore the Child God. Someone, way beyond the crests of the mountains, was watching and listening. Heaven was moving as well, while down below on earth, men and women were trying to reawaken the lost innocence of love in their own hearts.

Preparing the Cave

Father Anthony, the village priest, had rolled up his old cassock and was nailing some pieces of wood together. A few of the altar boys had offered to help him prepare the manger which was to be the cradle for the Baby Jesus.

Father Anthony was preparing the cave, just as Father Benjamin, the previous priest, had done, and the priest before him, Father Marcus, who had baptised all the grandparents of the village, and all previous priests before them. It is only those who live in the mountains who can boast of having a real cave for their Nativity scene.

And there was Martin, with a box of nails in his hands, repeating out loud one of the passages that Father Anthony had asked him to memorize.

"We rejoice with the angels, and we sing with our hearts because today the Son of God has been born in Bethlehem," recited the young boy.

The priest, without taking his eyes off the wood he was hammering, said to him: "That's fine, Martin! You are doing very well. That's enough for now. We will go over the rest when the Blessed Virgin and the shepherds arrive."

Father Anthony gave a final blow of the hammer and lifted up the manger as though he were making an offering to heaven. For Martin, working with wood was not unusual, accustomed as he was to wander about in the stables, but he smiled to see the priest savor his work of art, as if he had been chiseling away at some huge diamond.

"Doesn't it seem incredible that Almighty God becomes a baby and huddles on the straw which we are going to put in this manger? If you were God, would you do the same?" These questions came deep from the heart of this good priest. Martin and the other altar boys just looked on without saying anything. What could they say? Their silence was an act of awe and reverence which touched the greatness of this mystery.

The cave was to be the setting for the Nativity scene of the Holy Family after Midnight Mass. It was a family tradition that had passed from father to son, and everyone waited for this moment every year. Everyone gathered there to sing Christmas carols and to wish each other a happy Christmas. There was a shared sentiment among the people, just like there had been among the shepherds who heard the angels' announcement of the birth of Jesus. Who knows if some descendent of the shepherds had even come to live in this mountain village!

When the priest had asked Martin if he wanted to play the part of St. Joseph, Martin felt as though God himself was speaking to him. "Yes, of course!" he had answered, and only after the emotion of the moment had subsided did he see a small difficulty. "And who will be the Virgin Mary?"

This was an important question, because, like it or not, Martin and whoever it was going to be would have to get along well together, especially if they were to appear in public. "Ah! The Virgin...yes, well, it's going to be Beth, the baker's daughter."

Martin breathed a sigh that was a mixture of approval and relief. "Fine," he said. Until that moment he had never imagined the girl in the role of the Mother of God and even less as the wife of St. Joseph. It was just as well that they had been good friends since nursery school.

Looking at the cave, there was not much left to prepare. The manger was there, which was the important thing; St. Joseph and the Blessed Virgin needed one last practice, and they had to put on their tunics; the sacristan had been put in charge of getting the donkey, the ass, and a few lambs (which the people rivaled each other to give, each one saying his was the best); the children of the first Communion class were to dress as angels; other children, who were to be the shepherds, had nothing exceptional to do, because they were shepherds in real life. It was, therefore, an almost completely authentic representation.

Something Better than a Doll

Beth's house was the last one on the street, which wound its way up a rocky slope of the village. Martin was in a hurry to see her, but he had to take care not to slip because there were mirrors of ice hidden among the mounds of snow. He was still on his way when he heard her calling him from a window.

"Martin! Today's the day!" she told him, waving a blue handkerchief.

Martin went into her house and was immediately enveloped

by the friendly warmth of the fireplace. Beth's mother was known for her good-heartedness. It was rumored that her graceful hands were able in some miraculous way to multiply the bread that her husband baked in the ovens; that was the only explanation people had to explain the fact that she always had bread to give to others. It was not a rare sight to see her go into the houses of the village, giving out bread to the children and to families with old people, or sending bags of rolls with the mailman for the orphanage in the nearby village. Martin knew her well and within minutes was eating some of her delicious nut cakes.

On this occasion, Ellen, as Beth's mother was known, was absorbed in giving the last touches to the tunic that Beth was to wear. She was radiant with joy—even though she had slept very little the previous night.

"Mom, it's fine the way it is," repeated the girl, as her mother examined with minute care a picture card of the Virgin that she

was using as a design model. For a mother, it was a great source of holy pride to be able to dress one's own daughter as the Queen of Heaven. What would a woman not give to be the mother of the Mother of God! It would be impossible to describe what was going though Ellen's soul as she looked at her daughter Beth, who was to portray the beautiful face of the Virgin on Christmas night.

Martin held back a little. It was one of those moments when one knows one should be silent without having to be told. He waited with patience, but as the minutes passed by and the needle and thread kept moving in and out, he left discreetly and began to play with the younger children of the family. Children and games go together like salt and pepper. Even so, as a sign of the importance of the day, they all soon stopped playing and lent a hand to clear the entrance to the house of snow.

When Ellen had finished, Beth went to her room to change. A minute later she returned with the dress and gave it to her mother.

Martin asked her then if she wanted to go with him to see the manger that Father Anthony had just finished building.

"Can you come to my room for a moment?" was the only answer he received. If she had not given any importance to the manger, then it meant that something serious was on her mind. Martin followed her, and Beth closed the door behind him.

"What's going? Is there a problem with the dress? Are you going to tell me that you're not going to go ahead with this…?" Martin reacted like a frenzied cat.

"Hey, calm down! I haven't said anything yet. It's nothing like that." Martin breathed a sigh of relief. "It's about something I want to do, but I need you to tell me if Father Anthony will agree to it."

Martin, hearing that the priest was involved, became serious and attentive, like the good altar boy he was. Beth then took the toy figure of the baby and put it in Martin's arms.

"Well, then? What's wrong with the toy baby?" he asked in all innocence, giving it a little stroke on its nose. Beth's expression was not one of a girl about to have a tea party with her dolls.

"I think I understand," said Martin. Beth saw immediately that he did, and said, "And, instead of a doll, what if we bring a real baby?"

Martin immediately put the doll back in Beth's arms, perhaps feeling the difference between a plastic doll and a real baby, but suddenly he smiled and said, "What a great idea!"

They sat down and began to remember which families of the village had a baby at home. They dismissed the idea of asking the mayor's family, because their baby was two years old and nobody could control him; people said that he was a miniature tornado. Martin and Beth laughed at the idea that, instead of swaddling clothes, they'd have to wrap him up like an Egyptian mummy. Finally, they narrowed their list to six newborn babies.

They left the room and went to see Ellen. They told her of their idea, and she, seeing herself reflected in her daughter's eyes and brimming over with that goodness of hers, which the slightest motivation would arouse, embraced them both, showing her consent. Beth kissed her mother on both cheeks.

Father Anthony Learns of the Plan

They did not have much time. The children went skating across the frozen streets to look for Father Anthony, but they did not find him at the parish. The sacristan was brushing a donkey that had just come from a stable, and he told them that the priest had gone to speak with Joanne, the lady who had directed the village choir since her younger days. "Her younger days...." Martin was unable to imagine someone like Joanne ever being young; he had always thought of her as a living relic.

"You know what?" Martin said to the sacristan who had paused for a moment in his brushing. "Why don't you use the vacuum cleaner on him? It would be quicker!"...and Martin ran out as fast as lightning. There was a shout from the sacristan, and the horse's brush flew by Martin's ears. Beth ran with him, laughing. "Just as well that he threw the brush at *you* and not the donkey!" she said.

Heading towards Joanne's house, they saw that the priest was on his way back. He was protecting himself from the cold with a long cloak that covered him almost entirely. His black form stood out against the white snow. Martin thought that this was how Moses or David or Samson would have looked if they had lived in his mountain village.

"Good morning to St. Joseph and to his wife, the Blessed Virgin," he said with a smile and a small bow to them both. The two children looked at each other without saying anything, silently asking each other who would tell Father Anthony what they wanted to ask. Their silence made Father Anthony think that they had a secret to share. The priest took a step forward, and wrapped his cloak first around Martin and then Beth. "Well then, what's this all about?" he asked confidentially.

"We were thinking," began Beth, "that, if you agree, the Baby Jesus should be a *real* baby and not just a doll." Martin and Beth were surprised to see that the priest showed a quick sign of pleasure, like someone biting into a piece of his favorite cake.

"Whose idea was this?" he asked.

"Beth's."

"And you think the same, Martin?"

"Yes, yes…"

"Well, if I say no, will I have to start looking for statues of St. Joseph and the Blessed Virgin, or can I still count on both of you?"

The light in Beth's and Martin's eyes made any further questions unnecessary.

"Agreed!" they said in unison.

"But you both are in charge of finding the baby. Tell me what happens, because I need to know how everything will be in the cave," Father Anthony said.

"Thank you, Father Anthony! We will take care of everything."

It was almost noon. The sun did not let its rays penetrate the snow, as if not wanting to disturb it. The children rushed off to look for a real baby who would that very night be the Son of God. They were sure that if the people of the village were fiercely proud to have one of their children chosen to play the part of an angel or a shepherd, how much prouder someone would be if their baby could be in the hands of Mary and Joseph in the cave!

The footprints that Martin and Beth left in the snow were like freckles on the white face of the village.

The Six Infants

martin and Beth had their route worked out when they arrived at the village square. The six infants, according to their map, were the following:

Luke, the son of Ernest, the butcher

Robert, the son of Esther, the teacher

Louis, the son of Richard, the vet

Andrew, the son of John, the stonemason's handyman

Peter and Paul, the twins of Albert, the forest watchman

Martin had been an altar boy at the baptism of all of the infants, and he thought that it would be natural for the parents of the infants to want to give this little present to God. To Martin, it would be very ungrateful not to please God with this favor, seeing that he had made their infants into sons and citizens of heaven through baptism. What a great honor to have an infant rest in the arms of the Blessed Virgin after Midnight Mass!

After only an hour they had gone through all the streets of the village (it was a small village). Everything seemed to be against them! They could hardly believe what had just happened:

Luke was sick with a fever.

Robert was on his first family trip. He was going to spend Christmas in a cradle in his grandparents' house.

Louis had not slept all night, and his parents did not want to expose him to the night's cold air.

Andrew was crying his heart out because his mother was away.

Peter and Paul could not be separated. As soon as one of them felt the absence of the other, he gave a heart-piercing cry. The condition was to accept both of them or neither of them. But then, how could they have two infants as Baby Jesus?

Faced with this problem, Martin and Beth went to have a cup of hot tea so they could talk and try to figure out a solution.

"It was a good idea, Beth, but if it can't be done…. Don't worry, in the parish storeroom there are some old statues of saints. I will take the halo from one of the humble ones and put it on your doll. You'll see, everyone will think that it's the holy infant."

"It's not the same, Martin. You and I are not plastic statues, and neither are the shepherds, the angels, or the sheep or even the donkey."

"But what can we do?"

"I don't know, but I'm sure St. Joseph and the Virgin Mary will help us."

The tea was good, and they felt its warmth reach to the tips of their toes. For the moment there was nothing else to do but pray and wait for help from heaven.

They were just going into the church when a bell rang. They walked up to the altar and knelt down. Each made a heartfelt prayer to ask the parents of the Infant Jesus to find a baby. Martin remembered the story of Moses and how he saved his people from the Red Sea. He prayed in a straightforward and trusting way: "Dear God, will you help us find an infant and save him from the snow here in our village?"

They agreed to meet up after lunch. They would not give up. On Christmas Eve anything could happen. As they were leaving the church, the bell rang again and a white dove flew out of the bell tower. The two children were somehow sure that it was not just some frightened bird, but a messenger dove. They watched the dove fly away until they couldn't see it anymore, and they imagined God taking a rolled-up paper from the dove with their prayer written on it in golden letters.

The Shepherd, the Dove, and the Prayer to Mary

L unch was fast that day. It seemed that the cooking pots emptied themselves; it was as though they were under orders to put themselves as quickly as possible on the hot grill in order to let the delicious Christmas dinner have first place at the fire.

Martin's mother had kept the children's search for an infant to represent the Baby Jesus a secret. She quietly asked Martin to help her peel some potatoes and used this as an opportunity to ask him if he had found a family who would agree.

"No, Mom. The six babies in the village are sick, or away, or don't have permission. Do you know of any other family who has a baby?"

"I'm afraid not, dear. Aunt Lucy will have her child in a few weeks, and our neighbors Amy and Margaret won't have their babies until next month. And, you know, your next little brother will make us all happy in about six months' time!"

Martin was very happy to hear about his new brother. He gave his mother a hug and whispered softly, "Little brother, get ready, because next Christmas *you* will be the Infant Jesus." His mother hugged him even tighter, and Martin could almost hear a "Yes, I would love to" coming from the little heart of his unborn brother.

"Mom, I am off to the general rehearsal at the cave. Father Anthony is waiting for me."

"That's fine. Tell our reverend priest to take good care of my little St. Joseph."

Martin, upon leaving his house, saw a small, shaggy dog chasing a fat, plump cat. "What a coward that cat is!" he thought. He pulled on his red cap and walked to the end of the street where he met Beth.

"Hi! Any news?" Martin asked her.

"No, nothing, but I'm not giving up. Hey, do you want to go to the church through the field?"

"Sure, but you'll need to be careful when we jump over the stream, because the stones are icy. Do you remember when you fell in, and your father blamed me instead?"

"Don't exaggerate!" Beth said.

"I'm not exaggerating, but...."

"But what? If you're the one that falls into the stream this time, I will look for another St. Joseph."

"Would you really? Well, why don't we make a deal?" suggested Martin.

"What kind of a deal?"

"If one of us falls in, the other goes in as well, to help. Both of us dry, or both of us wet."

"Some gentleman you are! I hope St. Joseph is not listening!" Beth replied.

"Yes or no, Beth?"

"Okay!"

They took a path that led downhill along a stony, moss-covered wall. The shortcut did not save them much time, but for children a little bit of adventure can change a whole day.

There was a statue of Our Lady of Lourdes in a grotto at the foot of a majestic oak tree, built out of large, round stones. They stopped for a moment, as they always did, to pray a Hail Mary. The two children crossed their hands over their chests and, before be-

ginning their formal prayer, Beth offered an intention: "Holy Mother, help us to find an infant." The rush of nearby water accompanied her prayer.

Just as they said, "Amen," they were amazed to see the dove that had flown out of the church tower, perched on a branch of the tree. Because they were looking upwards, they did not realize that someone had come up behind them. Beth was the first to notice, and she immediately clutched Martin's arm.

"Good afternoon," said a nice-looking young man, dressed like a country shepherd.

"Good afternoon," they answered together.

"So you are going to be St. Joseph and the Blessed Virgin tonight after Mass?"

"Yes," answered Martin, "but how did you know?"

"Oh, it's not just me who knows! Here in the village and beyond, everyone knows," the young man said.

The children did not know who they were talking to, but they felt a familiar happiness in his presence. There was little difference in color between the young man's white tunic and the white snow which was everywhere. They could not tell which shone brighter.

"Is it true that you have not been able to find an infant to be the Baby Jesus in the cave?"

"It's true," said Martin. Beth continued, "We haven't found one yet, but we're going to keep looking until tonight."

There was a moment of silence, interrupted by the flutter of wings of the dove that flew off among the trees. This gave the children an opportunity to ask the young man a question.

"Excuse us, but are you from the village?" They felt something inside of them that was like being with a friend, even though they did not know the young man. They wanted to get to know him better.

"I am always here in the village, and when the dove flies it goes by my house. But that's not important. I'm here to give you both an answer to your request. At the end of Mass, Beth, don't go directly to the cave, but instead come back here as quickly as you can. Make sure you come from the other side of the stream, near the church. And bring the doll with you." "And then what should I do?" Beth asked.

The young man smiled and said in a soft voice: "You will know then. Now, here's something important: you should not mention to anyone what we have talked about, at least for the moment. Let's pray another Hail Mary."

The children knelt down in the snow, which was like a soft cusion for them, and they prayed. There was a smile on the Virgin's face. When they stood up they were alone. The shepherd had gone, just like the dove, without leaving any trace in the snow.

The Star over the Village

The rehearsal of the Nativity scene was not much more than just waiting around. There was not much to do or say. The only important thing was to make sure that each person knew exactly the moment to enter on the scene, where to stand, and when to leave. Father Anthony explained things well. Even so, he had to quiet two children who began to pull the meek donkey's tail. The donkey never complained.

Beth carried the doll in her arms, and neither she nor Martin said a word. They were still wondering about their meeting with the mysterious shepherd. As the rehearsal was finishing, Father Anthony told everyone to be very reverent at the Christmas Midnight Mass, especially the altar boys. He told them that the Nativity scene, which would be right after Mass, was a way to continue the happiness of having received the Child Jesus in holy Communion, and that it was one of the ways of welcoming his birth.

One girl raised her hand and asked, "Father, what part did you play when you were young?" The question caught the priest by surprise, but when he saw that everyone was interested, he answered, "The donkey!" The children's laughter echoed around the cave.

"No, that's not true, although I would have played that part very well! I had wanted to be St. Joseph, but I was given the part of a shepherd, just like most of you. I liked the part, and years later, when I was ordained a priest, I understood that the Infant Jesus wanted me to continue being a shepherd all my life."

This explanation was a sweet little drop of catechism for the children. One boy, with a lamb in his arms, cried out, "I want to be a shepherd too!" Only God knows if the boy's words were some small prophecy, and that perhaps this little man was a priest in the making, possibly even one day Father Anthony's successor.

The winter sun shed its last rays of light, and the few street decorations greeted the first evening stars. Everyone, including Father Anthony, eventually left the cave, leaving everything in silence, occasionally interrupted by the heavy breathing of the donkey and the bleating of a few lambs. Everyone had gone home for Christmas dinner.

Martin and Beth walked together until their paths separated. Each reminded the other of what the young man had told them: "Do not mention to anyone what we have talked about, at least for the moment."

All the families of the village were celebrating the Infant Jesus soon to be born. There were colored lights, laughter, songs, the sounds of joy, and even the odd firecracker. When the sun finally set behind the mountain, a star that had never before been seen began to shine. No one noticed it. A ray from the star shone down and touched one side of the mountain. It silhouetted the shadow of a man and a woman, on a donkey, making their ponderous way towards the village.

Christmas Midnight Mass

The church's new outdoor lighting was turned on for the first time that night. The mayor was proud of the council's contribution, while the priest said that the faith of the people lit up not only the front entrance of the church, but their own hearts as well. Church and hearts, all was lit up for the beginning of Midnight Mass.

The altar boys were running riot in the sacristy. They were like so many twittering birds nervous before a sudden storm. The poor

boys received orders from all sides: from the sacristan, the catechism teachers, Joanne the choir directress, and from a few mothers who were giving last-minute instructions. It felt like a chaotic birdcage until Father Anthony came to put on his priestly vestments. His very presence imposed silence and serenity. With his fatherly look and a few kind words, he made everyone understand that Mass was about to begin. He said something that the adults especially understood: "Martha has worked well; now it is time for Mary's better part."

The altar boys lined up for the entrance procession. Martin carried the thurible, something he loved to do. Father Anthony discreetly approached him and asked him in a low voice how the search for the baby had ended. Martin hesitated for an instant and then answered, "Everything worked out fine." Just then, the bell master pulled the ropes, and a bust of joy announced the procession.

Everyone from the village was in the church. Joanne produced the finest from her musical repertoire, and the songs traveled up the bell tower and ran off along the most distant mountain paths.

Father Anthony's sermon touched the hearts of all. He preached like a real shepherd who, ever since he had been a boy, had accompanied the Infant Jesus on this happy night of Christmas. Was his sermon long or short? Nobody asked, because no one missed a single word. His main message was that each person's heart was like a cradle in which Jesus would be born. What a joy for each heart to be a cradle for the world's Redeemer!

The moment arrived for the consecration of the bread and wine into the body and blood of Our Lord. The altar boys were kneeling around the altar, and Martin, in the center, sprinkled incense around the host. "Jesus," he prayed, "how nice it is to be with you. I wish you a happy Christmas. Accept my heart as your cradle." The scent of the incense filled his lungs. At the end of the consecration the people stood up, and the noise made by the benches hid something that only Martin and Beth saw: the white dove was perched on a rafter of the roof of the church.

Mass continued solemnly until the end. Once again in the sacristy, the altar boys left their cassocks and surplices to go full speed to prepare the Nativity scene in the cave. Someone asked for Beth, and Martin answered that she was on her way. Yes, she was on her way, but only Martin knew that she was "on her way" not to the cave but to the field—on her way to find out heaven's answer to their prayers.

The Newborn Child

"After Midnight Mass, Beth, you will not go directly to the cave. Instead you will come quickly to this field, but from the other side, near the church. And bring the doll with you...."

The small girl ran, scarcely watching where she stepped. It was curious that she did not hit anything, nor did she slip on the ice-covered stones. It was as if she were running fast over an open field covered with flowers.

She stopped in front of the young man dressed in white. She had arrived on time! The young man made an elegant gesture, asked her for the doll, and indicated that she should go on ahead. She did so, slowly. She took two, three, four steps, until her gaze fell on a beautiful young woman, seated on a tree stump with a child in her arms. There was a man standing there, too, beside a donkey.

Beth joined her hands and knelt down. The young woman said to her, "I am very happy to see you. My child has been born and wants to be with you and Martin, and with everyone else in this mountain village."

Beth heard these words in her ears, but it was her heart that was filled by them. Her love for God and her trust in the Holy Virgin made her live this extraordinary event with the same simplicity with which she said a prayer before going to sleep.

Her lips scarcely opened to say the words, "Don't you want to come with me?"

The Virgin smiled sweetly and answered, "I will be there, but I would like my son to rest in your arms. He loves the affection and goodness of your heart. He will also be happy for your loved ones to receive him."

There was nothing to compare with Beth's joy when the Virgin Mary held out her arms and gave the newborn Child to her. He was asleep. Holding the Child, Beth felt the same inner peace that filled her soul when she received holy Communion from Father Anthony's hands. The Child felt the warmth of a heart that welcomed him and nestled trustingly in her arms.

The Virgin spoke again: "It is time to return to the church and go to the cave. They are waiting for us!"

Beth stood up. Not wanting to look away, she took a step backwards. The image of the Virgin Mary and St. Joseph and the donkey all faded away. She turned around and suddenly found herself at the entrance to the cave. That was very strange, but Beth seemed not to notice. The joy of holding the Child surpassed any capacity for surprise.

Martin was the first to notice that Beth had arrived and ran to meet her. Everything had happened so quickly! Little St. Joseph stared at the Child; he could hardly believe his eyes. Then Beth, dressed in dignity as the Virgin Mary, saw that the Baby opened his eyes and looked at her for the first time. He held up his little arms, and she kissed him as she held him tightly. Martin also kissed him and put one of the Child's tiny hands to his face, rubbing it on his fake beard.

Nothing needed to be explained to anyone. The children who were dressed as shepherds and angels entered the cave, followed by Martin and Beth, with the Infant Jesus in her arms.

Adeste Fideles

Joanne gave the signal to the choir, and everyone began to sing the Christmas hymn *Adeste Fideles*. The great star stayed in the sky over the cave, and it seemed so near that its rays shone as bright (or maybe even brighter) as the moon itself.

Father Anthony, still dressed in his solemn vestments, was there at the Nativity scene with the people. An unexpected joy filled the hearts of all who were present. Even the small children were quiet, something that did not happen on most occasions. Tiredness and sleep had disappeared. Everyone sang, except Martin and Beth, who gazed on the Child who had come from heaven to be with them.

Just like when Jesus was a young man and most people saw him merely as "the son of the carpenter," on this occasion everyone, even the priest, saw only a baby in Beth's arms. Even so, the mystery of the divine presence in swaddling clothes was perceived in some way by each person, according to his or her own particular measure of faith and love.

Christmas hymns were sung in Gregorian chant, with prayers led by the Father Anthony and popular Christmas carols all intertwined without pause.

What the little St. Joseph and the Virgin Mother could not hear was the conversation of each person with the Christ Child. As always, the greatest miracles are not touched or seen or heard….

They are scarcely perceived, because God likes to work secretly on the conversion and sanctity of each person's soul. There were some changes of heart that were not written down or heard, but they remained as special Christmas presents in that mountain village:

* Jeremy promised the Child Jesus that he would be a patient and responsible father. He asked forgiveness for not always having been a loving husband, and for the times he had not listened to his children.

* Little Lucy had been somewhat jealous of her younger sister and had not helped her mother to take care of her. She told the Child Jesus that she would look after her little sister just as the Virgin had looked after him.

＊ Jacob had a thorn in his soul. When he was fifteen years old he had been disloyal. He had blamed the loss of a sum of money on his cousin, even though it was Jacob who had been responsible for putting the money in an envelope that had been thrown into the fire by mistake. He asked forgiveness of the Child Jesus and planned to make things right.

＊ The immaculate purity of the Holy Family entered deeply into the heart of Francis. He received the grace of sincere forgiveness and was ready, after a long time, to confess his sins and begin a life worthy of his Christian dignity.

＊ Elizabeth was a good girl, but she had not taken life very seriously. Her parents were worried about her, but she had not listened to them. The beauty and humility of God become man touched her sensibility and made her reconsider things. That very night she would return home, arm in arm with her parents, asking them how she might become a good mother, if that was what the Lord wanted.

✳ Julie was preparing for her first Communion, but she had not made her best effort to learn her catechism. Not only that; she was waiting for May only to remind her parents that she wanted a big celebration. The Child Jesus made her see that in order to receive him into her heart, she needed to be humble and generous and think of others before herself, just as he had done. The girl promised to be the first to learn all her catechism, and she vowed that she would be a good girl, not concerned with presents for herself, but rather with being a present herself for others.

As St. John the Evangelist said, "If one were write down everything that was said in the secret of people's hearts, a whole library would not be sufficient."

The last hymn was again *Adeste Fideles.* The little shepherds received a sign from Father Anthony to take their presents and offer them to the Holy Family. They left fruit, flowers, clothes, vegetables, bread, and even toys in the simple wicker baskets that had been provided. Then Martin (little St. Joseph) picked up a basket decorated with golden ribbons and went down among everyone.

Some time ago, the priest had had the good idea of asking the village carpenters to cut pieces of wood in the shape of hearts. On the third Sunday of Advent, he gave them out at the end of Mass with the following invitation: "Let us give the Child Jesus a welcome in our hearts; those who want to can write their names on these pieces of wood; each wooden heart will be a symbol of our welcome, as beautiful as the cradle."

The basket was filling up, but Martin did not feel its weight. The wooden hearts were made light by love. The last person to put his heart in the basket was Roger, the stonemason, who by then was a little pale because he almost could not find it in his pockets.

The great star beamed bright when the priest addressed the families to give them the final blessing. The white dove flew in and perched on a piece of wood near the donkey. The little lambs bleated, and all the people moved aside so that the children could leave the cave. Martin and Beth walked slowly, without stopping. Everyone else stayed behind to wish each other a happy Christmas. They did not notice that the children had headed towards the field, or that they had not gone to the parish hall to change.

"Thank You!"

St. Joseph and the Blessed Virgin were waiting for the children. There was a winding mountain path behind them; it was lit up by the silver light of the Christmas star. Martin and Beth had not taken off their tunics, so when they arrived with the Baby Jesus it seemed as though each saint had its own little twin.

"We don't know how to thank you," said Beth, stretching out her arms. The Virgin took the Child and kissed him very tenderly.

"All our thanks is to Our Lord, who looks contentedly on our humility," replied the Virgin. Nature itself seemed to echo the sweet tone of her voice, and the sounds from the village celebrations seemed to fade gently into the distance. The children's conversation was a prayer. Martin, still wearing his fake beard, said, "Don't you want to stay at our house?"

Big St. Joseph, the real one, gave him a hug and, with a glance at his wife, said, "Martin…or should I say 'little Joseph?'…you are very kind, but we are staying with you all. That's why there is peace now in everyone's heart, thanks to both of you. And that's the meaning of Christmas, isn't it?"

The donkey bowed down a little, and St. Joseph helped the Virgin to sit on his back. The night was offering its brightest stars, and with the village lit up, it seemed to the children that it was the best setting for a Christmas scene they had ever seen.

St. Joseph took the reigns of the donkey, much bigger than the donkey in the cave, and grasped his staff. Martin and Beth drew

near to the Virgin to see the Infant Jesus once again. They caressed him; he opened his eyes, took Martin's finger, and smiled.

"He is so beautiful!" said the Virgin, and Beth added, "Yes, he resembles you."

There was no hurry to say good-bye, but inside the children felt from that moment on that they both had an important part in bringing the Child Jesus to all men and women. The donkey still had to travel around the world—and also St. Joseph, on foot. Therefore, they only asked for a good-bye kiss. St. Joseph left the reigns, approached them, and lifted them up near the Virgin.

The Holy Family was on its way again. Martin and Beth glanced at each other and, understanding each other's look, ran to either side of the Holy Family. They wanted to give the Holy Family a token of remembrance. Martin took his red cap out of his bag and gave it to St. Joseph; Beth took off the blue scarf she was wearing and gave it to Mary.

"Thank you—thank you both very much."

The children turned around and walked a few steps, but they could not help looking back to follow with their eyes these holy persons whom they loved.

When all that remained was a silhouette on the snowy background of the mountain, the two children took each other's hands and ran all the way to the village.

St. Joseph's Cap

martin arrived home dressed as St. Joseph. He was so happy and smiling that his mother did not ask him where he had been. What family had given them their infant for the presentation? It did not seem right to ask. When heaven touches earth, all questions already seem to be answered.

By now, Alex was asleep in bed. Martin put on his pajamas and went out of his room to sit for a moment in front of the crèche. He did not turn on the light. The last pieces of wood were burning in

the fireplace and giving out their last few flames, which threw dancing shadows around the room. Little lights illumined the Nativity scene, and the boy fixed his gaze on St. Joseph.

How beautiful it had been to meet him! He felt proud to have played the part of St. Joseph in the cave. He was not as old as some people had painted him, and he was much more fun than people could have imagined.

"He will look after the Virgin and the Child Jesus well," he murmured to himself.

He heard a few steps and turned around. It was Alex. Wasn't he fast asleep, just like a stuffed teddy bear?

"What's up? Weren't you asleep?" Martin asked.

"Yes, I was, but I'm awake now." Alex sat down and blew on the embers, which shot up a big flame. The hot light reddened their faces.

"Alex," said Martin, "are you happy?" This obvious question

seemed out of place, but it was important for the boy to hear the answer.

"Why do you ask? Aren't you?... Of course I am! I am so happy that I woke up to be able to laugh with you. Do you want to hear something?"

"Yes, of course—whatever."

"Well, when I was asleep I dreamed that I was in the cave again, clapping at the Nativity scene tonight. I clapped so hard that my hands hurt. You were there, but suddenly I saw another you—I mean the real St. Joseph—and he made me laugh because he was wearing your cap on his head."

Martin, who was already filled with so many reasons to be happy, felt something like an electric shock run through him from top to bottom upon hearing his little brother's story. He spontaneously hugged his little brother, who was a bit taken aback.

"Wait! Didn't you like my dream?"

"Of course I did! I loved it, but it's late now and I don't want to wake up Mom and Dad. Why don't we go back to sleep so that you can go on dreaming funny things?"

"Okay!"

"Let's go then, and tomorrow, if you want to, you can wake me up with your frog."

As he was closing his eyes, Martin prayed from the depth of his heart: "Jesus, Mary, and Joseph, I give you my heart and my soul. Jesus, Mary, and Joseph, help me at my final hour. Jesus, Mary, and Joseph, let my soul rest in peace."

The Virgin Mary's Scarf

That steep path had always been difficult to climb, especially when it was covered with snow. But Beth ran along it just like a squirrel. She arrived home radiant with happiness, but at the same time with a quietness of manner that was unusual for her. The whole family was still up: her parents, her older brothers, and little Christine. "Oops! I'm very late," Beth thought. Everyone reached out to hug and kiss her. They had all been waiting to share their family-size happiness with her.

Her mother Ellen had hot tea ready for Beth, with a few drops of lemon, just the way she liked it. Everyone was talking about how beautiful the Mass had been, how well Father Anthony had preached, and also how they had felt the presence of God in the cave. Beth's family made one think of those shepherds at the very first Nativity scene, filled with humility and joy and brimming with faith and goodness of heart.

Then they all began to go off to bed. Beth was heading to her room when she remembered that she had forgotten something very important. She quickly returned to the Nativity scene and picked up the little statue of the Baby Jesus. She caressed it softly in her hands and kissed it.

"What are you doing?" asked her mother.

"Mom, I'm kissing the Baby Jesus. Do you want to kiss him too?"

"Yes, with all my heart," and Ellen bent down to her daughter.

She kissed the statue and also Beth's forehead.

"Mom, I haven't told you, but...." she began in a confidential tone.

"The baby? What a beautiful baby!.... Now, what do you want to tell me? You don't need to say anything, dear, because we mothers know all about babies. Why not just keep the peace and happiness of today like a great treasure all your life? You don't know all that went through my heart seeing you as the Virgin Mary tonight. I felt as though the Virgin herself were telling me: 'Don't you see how your daughter takes after me?'"

Beth listened without saying a word. They had prayed together many times, but now it seemed that heaven itself had come in through the door and windows. Her mother continued, motioning toward her room, "Dearest, take care of the Baby Jesus in your heart, just as you held him today in your arms. In that way I will continue hearing from the Virgin in my prayers that she is happy with you. And something else, too. We mothers understand each other in a special way. I listen to what the Virgin Mother tells me in my heart to help me love and educate my children."

They hugged each other tightly, ever so tightly. Tears began to fill the little girl's eyes. She went into her room and went over to the window to see the great star one more time. She saw that it was now shining over another mountain. She waved. At that moment she saw a shadow cross the silver sky and head towards her. She opened the window, and the fresh air blew her hair. The familiar dove was perched on the windowsill, and she stroked him.

Beth took him in her hands and noticed that he had a string tied to one of his feet. She took the string, and her heart again jumped for joy. The messenger dove, who had now just flown off, had brought her a little thread from her white scarf.

A Gift from God

The last person to go to sleep that night in the village was Father Anthony, although that night he had fallen asleep in the church. There he was, sitting up, asleep, with his head bowed slightly forward. After the Nativity play—that is, after the visit of the Infant Jesus to his faithful—Father Anthony had gone straight to the Nativity scene at one side of the altar for a few moments of prayerful contemplation.

The outside of the church was still lit up, but inside only the sanctuary lamp and the colored lights of the Nativity scene flickered. The good priest, having guided his flock to the one Good Shepherd, fell asleep. He slept with a happy heart, because the angels had passed throughout the village announcing the birth of the Messiah, and the church had been full like never before.

And the child that Beth and Martin had brought? It remained a mystery, like so many other mysteries that decorated his church with faith and hope. Of one thing he was certain: The Child Jesus had touched the soul of each person, and they had welcomed him. There was no greater satisfaction for a man consecrated to God in the priesthood.

It was cold in the church. Father Anthony was huddled over, his arms apparently folded. So much happiness had worn him out. The manger that he had built with his own hands had become a chest for his greatest treasure: "A Child has been born to us...God has visited his people."

The young man with the snow-white tunic drew near to the good priest and covered him with a woolen blanket. He then left on the straw a Christmas present from God for his good friend: a heart of gold.

HAPPY CHRISTMAS!